For Hannah and Iola, to inspire wild wonder
in your urban adventures, with love. CB

For Josie. CE

First published in Great Britain in 2026 by Otter-Barry Books,
Little Orchard, Burley Gate, Herefordshire, HR1 3QS
www.otterbarrybooks.com info@otterbarrybooks.com

A catalogue record for this book is available from the British Library.

ISBN 978-1-915659-80-4

Illustrated with mixed media
Set in Alegreya Sans and Mr Dodo

Printed in China

1 3 5 7 9 8 6 4 2

Authorised Representative: Easy Access System Europe – Mustamäe tee 50, 10621 Tallinn, Estonia,
gpsr.requests@easproject.com

FSC www.fsc.org
MIX
Paper | Supporting responsible forestry
FSC® C104723

CITIES going wild

...to save the planet

Written by CATHERINE BARR
Illustrated by CHRISTIANE ENGEL

Otter-Barry BOOKS

Contents

Introduction

By 2050, two out of every three people on Earth will probably live in cities. In this book you will tour the world, meeting wildlife that is also settling into city life.

You will find out how bringing nature back into cities is helping people as well as the planet. You will discover sponge cities, bird-friendly cities, living seawalls, high-rise forests, pollinator pathways and guerrilla gardens.

You will see how nature brings joy, health, wildlife and, critically, resilience to climate change in our increasingly urban world.

From cherry orchards over motorway junctions to skyscraper peregrine nests, wonderful wetland walkways and pangolin pathways, turn these pages to peek into some of the world's greenest urban jungles.

"Cities are where the Climate Battle will largely be won or lost."
António Guterres, United Nations Secretary-General

Bird-Friendly Cities

Migrating birds look out for green spaces and sparkling blue waters to rest and feed. But around the world, cities in their paths are spreading upwards in glass and outwards in concrete. Birds navigating at night are confused by city lights and billions fly into skyscrapers.

But flocks will avoid bird-friendly glass, with special marks they can see and swerve. In an urban sprawl, these flying visitors need a network of wild patches and fewer lights, so they can navigate with stars by night.

City park nesting boxes in Singapore encourage hornbills to settle and stay.

Burrowing Owls go underground in Phoenix, Arizona, USA, in a transformed city rubbish dump.

Bird-friendly designs help birds stay safe at the Orange Cube, Lyon, France.

Shy Pacific Great Blue Herons get used to people in a busy park in Vancouver, Canada.

In bird-friendly cities, birds find insects to pick off grassy roofs, make homes in nesting boxes, discover peace in tiny gardens and shade in tree-lined paths and streets.

From seagulls far from European shores to exotic parrots, Burrowing Owls and spectacular birds of prey, birds are swooping in, and many settle into city life.

Peregrine Falcons move onto Battersea Power Station, London, UK.

Be a budding birder!

Put up a nesting box, a bird feeder or water to drink - if possible, at home and at school.

High-Rise Tweets

Central Park, New York City, USA

In Spring and Autumn, there is a busy bird highway in the skies over New York City. Songbirds, shorebirds, seabirds and birds of prey migrate along the Atlantic Flyway, heading south down the North American coast. Listen out and look up to see Brent Geese arriving from the Arctic for winter, and honking Snow Geese. Twice a year migrating flocks funnel through Central Park.

Bird visitors like Yellow-Rumped Warblers meet permanent park residents like the pretty Northern Flicker and the American Robin. Spy New York's famous Red-Tailed Hawks. Beyond the trees, one bird slices through the concrete jungle after pigeons. This Peregrine Falcon is the world's fastest flying bird.

Can you spot these birds?

Yellow-Rumped Warbler

Brent Goose

Snow Goose

Peregrine Falcon

Northern Shoveler

Red-Tailed Hawk

American Robin

Spongy Spaces

Beneath forests, soil soaks up rainwater like a sponge. But in cities, rainwater cannot sink into concrete, so stormwaters sweep rubbish and sewage along in dangerous, dirty floods.

But some cities are creating green spaces so rainwater soaks in rather than runs off. These sponge cities are turning urban jungles into wetland wonders.

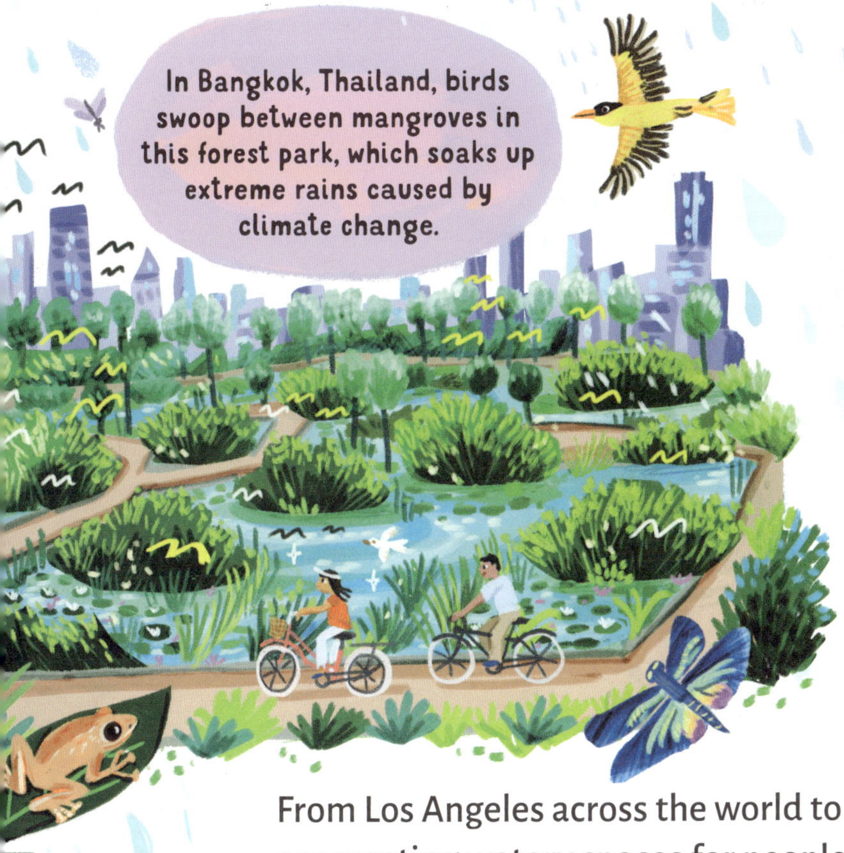

From Los Angeles across the world to Berlin, sponge cities are creating watery spaces for people and wildlife. Wide roadside flower beds, rain playgrounds, ponds, cool, tree-lined paths, lakes and parks are all breaking apart a sea of concrete.

Birds, insects and other water-loving wildlife are flooding back into these cities, where rain brings joy in wilder, wetter city spaces.

Be a sponge spotter!

How spongy is your city or your street? Draw a map of all the green spaces near your home.

Wild, Wet Wonders

Wetland park in Sanya Dong'an, China

Water-loving snakes slither and frogs squelch through Sanya Dong'an's wetland park. They live in a beautiful river park that carves through this Chinese city, once clogged with pollution and damaged by dangerous floods.

In this spongy city, monsoon rains now flow into rice fields and streams. Banyan trees grow on lake islands, their leaves spreading welcome shade.

Here snowy-white egrets paddle through ponds, hares sip sparkling waters and beady-eyed herons are on the look-out for fish.

In this watery city paradise, you can run along skywalks in the canopy and spot skyscrapers that rise out of the trees. On scorching summer days you can play in this wet, beautiful playground and keep cool under a canopy of leaves.

Can you spot these creatures?

Pond Heron

Snowy Egret

Greater Green Snake

Riffle Beetle

Rana Spinulosa Frog

Hainan Hare

Living Walls

In some cities there are skyscrapers built for trees, where people live behind curtains of leaves. Trees on balconies and plants on window sills soak up rain and give shade. They suck up city dust and muffle traffic noise.

Flowers and grasses are also planted on specially made roofs. These living roofs create habitats for birds, butterflies, grasshoppers and even lizards.

The seaside city of Plymouth, UK, is turning lifeless concrete seawalls into green, underwater homes at high tide for a biodiversity bonanza of seaweeds, shrimps, fish and oysters.

Living walls can also go down under the sea. In some coastal cities, people are creating homes for creatures on the slippery sea walls that divide the city from the ocean. These artificial homes replace lost saltwater habitats, once busy with animals and seaweeds that thrive in tides and lapping waves.

Even buses and bus shelters can add a splash of colour that encourages nature to settle into the city, in Singapore.

In Amsterdam, The Netherlands, green roofs are planted with flowers and food that insects, birds and people will all enjoy.

Be a high-rise gardener!

If you have space on your windowsill, perhaps you can plant wildflowers in a window box to attract insects and birds to your city view!

Creatures in Crevices

Sydney, Australia

Sydney Harbour in Australia is a pioneer city for Living Seawalls around the world. Hundreds of different types of sea creatures are moving back into new, high-rise, watery spaces. These new seawall homes come in ten shapes and sizes. Each of them creates different habitats attracting different creatures.

There are tiny rock pools, knobbly surfaces called 'sponge fingers', honeycombs where animals can hide from predators, open shapes that small fish like blennies can swim through – and others, like the kelp holdfasts, that they can attach to.

Visitors can get close to take a look and see how biodiversity is being boosted in this shoreline city. Once the tiny animals have settled in, scientists hope sea turtles, seahorses and seals will once more investigate these rocky, food-rich shores.

Can you spot these sea creatures?

Southern Pygmy Leatherjacket

Shore Crab

Rock Oyster

Green Sea Turtle

Anemone

White's Seahorse

Australian Fur Seal

Garden Cities

Creating space for plants helps wildlife move back into cities. Trees are home to birds, butterflies and other insects, but they also suck pollution from dirty city air. This makes cooler, cleaner and healthier spaces for people too.

From mini-forests to tiny gardens, from wild, roadside verges to cleaned-up rivers, grey, polluted city spaces are being given the chance to go green.

Sky gardens in Tokyo, Japan, awash with cherry blossom, arch over a motorway loop, bringing birds to its fragrant pink branches.

Wildlife thrive and people feel better in greener cities. In New York, children get a bird's eye view from the High Line, a high-rise nature path. In Izmir, Turkey, people relax in parklets, amongst groups of potted plants. In Tokyo, pink cherry trees loop over a motorway junction in a sky garden.

Whether low-rise or high-rise, nature gives biodiversity and people a boost.

in Mumbai, India, communities are planting mini-forests in small spaces to create canopies of green in the heart of this crowded city.

Families cycle between parks in Vienna, Austria, a super-green European city, where more than half of the city space is green.

Be a guerrilla gardener!

In spring, look out for patches of city soil to sprinkle wildflower seeds. Whether around a tree or between the paving, revisit your guerrilla garden to water it and celebrate its blooms.

City in Nature

Singapore

Singapore is the world's first 'city in nature' – an urban oasis where lush plants curl up skyscrapers and pink speckled orchids decorate energy-making solar Supertrees. These artificial trees are vertical gardens that turn sunlight into energy and collect rainwater too.

Singapore's many parks are connected by green corridors, grown to mimic forest layers with butterfly-friendly plants and canopies rich with insects for birds.

Tropical birds flit across rich green parks and frogs hop in and out of ponds. Rare pangolins amble across wildlife bridges over highways into the city through protected forest parks.

The endangered Smooth-Coated Otter has returned to Singapore's meandering city rivers, once concrete canals. Gardens across the city encourage people to enjoy nature as part of urban life.

Can you spot these creatures?

Blue-Throated Bee Eater

Blue-Crowned Hanging Parrot

Pangolin

Smooth-Coated Otter

Common Green-Back Toad

Olive-Backed Sunbird

Pollinator Pathways

Bees and other insects pollinate most of the food we eat. In the countryside, farming pesticides are killing bees but in cities, if there are enough flowers to feed from, wild bees can thrive.

Colourful urban spaces bloom with bee-friendly flowers and create pathways for pollinators. Butterflies, moths, hoverflies and bees alight to feed in messy, wilder spaces, however small.

More and more cities are planting insect super-highways. Pollinators fly from city gardens, along uncut road verges, spotting flowery window boxes and buzzing around allotments and parks. They discover bug hotels built by bumblebee-caring communities, who are now sharing stories of these tiny flower-loving city dwellers around the world.

On the John Muir Pollinator Path in Edinburgh, Scotland, UK, the B-Line passes through parks, road verges and school grounds, all being transformed into colourful, flower-filled havens.

Wild pollinators and bumblebees are settling into small spaces created in Bumblebee-friendly UK schools buzzing for Bronze, Silver and Gold Awards.

Win a Bumblebee Award!

Inspire your school to go wildflower-mad and win a Bumblebee-friendly Schools Award. Plant flowers that bees love. Build a bug hotel so they stop and stick around.
bumblebeeconservation.org

The Urban Buzz

Oslo, Norway

In Oslo, wild pollinators such as solitary bees fly across the city from flower to flower on a pioneering Bee Highway. They sip nectar from bee-friendly, local flowers planted by schools, businesses and local people.

This pollinator pathway has created a buzz and there are now a growing number of bee-friendly cities around the world.

Wild pollinators buzz in and out of underground homes, deadwood and specially built insect hotels. Honey Bees are looked after by urban beekeepers who harvest and sell their delicious honey.

This helps people to understand bees better, to enjoy healthy honey and also learn about the important role of wild pollinators like Bumblebees, moths and butterflies.

Can you spot these insects?

Red Mason Bee

Common Blue Butterfly

Honey Bee

Green Forester Moth

Tree Bumblebee

Nature-Ways

Planting trees along streets into cities helps funnel cool air into sizzling cities. In Seoul in South Korea these wind paths are turning down the heat, and in Medellin in Colombia more than 30 green corridors help to keep this city cool.

Nature corridors connect green spaces, making it easier for wildlife to journey around the city, finding enough food and mates.

A network of nature means migrating animals and birds can stay on the move. In Asia, bridges built for wildlife are helping pangolins cross the road, while in Canada and Alaska, USA, green bridges and tunnels are guiding bigger animals like moose away from city traffic and people too.

Nature paths help wildlife stay safe, so people and wildlife can live together in an urban jungle.

Beavers have been reintroduced in West London, where it is hoped one day they will recreate watery pathways and pools rich with life in the urban landscape.

Cool mountain air flows into Seoul, South Korea's capital, through specially planted wind paths.

Moose choose to wander through a tunnel to avoid the traffic in Anchorage, Alaska, USA.

Be a green way finder!

Use a local map to discover the ways to walk, roller-skate or cycle between green spaces. You may find a footpath or a bicycle path or even a tow path that avoids busy, more polluted road routes.

Ribbons of Blue

Birmingham, UK

The world's longest community orchard stretches for 50 miles along the canals through the city of Birmingham in the UK. As they grow, the fruit trees will bring bees, birds, butterflies and bats along city waterways once clogged with waste.

Today playful otters steal fish from garden ponds while damselflies and skimming insects cruise wildflower-fringed canals. Birmingham is planting to become one of the world's most environmentally friendly cities.

Birmingham is the UK's first Nature City, celebrating urban communities with more nature and better green spaces. It is also part of a global network of green cities that put nature first.

From hedgerows to rivers, from tree-lined streets to cleaned-up canals, communities are working together to connect nature. And they are getting help and sharing ideas from other super-green cities around the world.

Can you spot these creatures?

Mallard Duck

Eurasian Otter

Peacock Butterfly

Brown Long-Eared Bat

Common Blue Damselfly

White-Tailed Bumblebee

Urban Jungle Food

It's a challenge for people in cities to eat fresh, local food grown to boost health and nature. Using pesticides, factory-farming animals, transporting food long distances and throwing away wasted food all add to pollution and increase poor health.

Cities are exploring different ways to grow food in the urban jungle. Businesses are sprouting salads in skyscrapers. This vertical farming means growing food on shelves inside, using less land and destroying less nature. Cities around the world are working together to share ideas, train gardeners and grow vegetables so people can eat healthy, local food.

In Havana, Cuba, 90% of the city's food is grown in the city, with organic fruit and veg at a price that locals can afford.

In Los Angeles, USA, Ron Finley, also known as the Gangsta Gardener, started growing food in his parkway and it has sparked a food-growing revolution of Californian community gardens.

Local volunteers in Budapest, Hungary, have transformed an old car park into a food forest of edible plants..

From edible food forests to community gardens, colourful allotments, school vegetable plots, roadside verges and seed banks for local people, people are finding all sorts of different ways to grow greens.

These food patches bring butterflies, bugs, bees and birds. In these peaceful places, people grow, eat and share super-healthy food!

Children in Antananarivo, Madagascar, are eating fresher, better food from vegetables grown in old rice sacks at school.

In Shanghai, China, leafy greens like lettuce and spinach are thriving in huge, undercover vertical farms.

Grow food to share!

Plant a micro-garden at home or at school! You only need a small space or some pots to grow salad vegetables like lettuce leaves, basil, radishes and even nasturtiums to create colourful meals. Adding edible flowers like nasturtiums and pansies is fun, especially in salads to share.

Tiny, Edible Gardens
Dakar, Senegal

Africa has the fastest-growing urban population in the world. On market tables and in small city spaces, people across the West African city of Dakar are growing food to feed their communities.

Fertile soil and land around the city is scarce but in these micro-gardens, people are growing food without needing soil. Instead, they are using local waste by recycling peanut shells, coconut fibres and sand.

A network of micro-gardens is cared for by women, young people and the elderly. These tiny and productive gardens are even sprouting in city prisons.

People are learning new gardening skills and over 10,000 people have now learned to grow their own food. Families are eating more healthily and micro-gardens are spreading in other cities too.

Can you spot these foods?

Lettuce

Watermelon

Mango

Sweetcorn

French Beans

Glossary

Animal superhighway
A pathway that many animals regularly use over time.

Biodiversity
The variety of life on Earth.

Canopy
The leaves and branches of the highest layer of a rainforest.

Climate change
Changes in world weather, most recently caused by human activities such as burning fossil fuels.

Deadwood
Parts or all of a tree that has died.

Guerrilla-gardening
Growing flowers, fruit or vegetables in public spaces where you do not have permission, such as abandoned land, often to benefit local communities.

Habitat
A natural environment that is home to living things.

Micro-gardens
Fruit and vegetables grown in small, specially designed city spaces or containers.

Migration
The movement of living things from one place to another.

Monsoon
Winds of the Indian Ocean that bring seasons of heavy rain.

Navigation
The way of working out how to get from one place to another.